# Spirit-led Soulwinning

by

ERWIN COOK

Imaginary Press
1233 Pennsylvania Avenue
Dalton, GA 30720
www.imaginarypress.com

Ordering Information:
Quantity sales. Special discounts are available on quantity purchases by corporations, associations, and others. For details, contact the publisher at the address above.
Orders by U.S. trade bookstores and wholesalers. Please contact Big Distribution: Tel: (800) 800-8000; Fax: (800) 800-8001 or visit www.bigbooks.com.

Printed in the United States of America

# CONTENTS

# Chapter 1:
# What's Happening

My name is Erwin. I was raised in a Baptist church. My dad left my mother when I was at a young age. My mother was in and out of marriages when I was growing up. I grew up with one brother. My mom use to work a lot while raising us boys. I remember one time we met this wonderful family in the church. They took me in and started to babysit me when I was around seven.

I first got baptized in the church and accepted the Lord as my personal Savior. I was living in Dalton, Georgia, at the time. Not having a dad in my life, I learned about life and how to be a man from church and school. Then later on, my mother took us to Fort Oglethorpe, where I attended school.

I got out of going to church as we moved on. I started to get in with the wrong crowds, joining gangs in middle school. I remember that on my first day of school, I was doing acid I bought from my friends.

The next thing I knew, I took a field trip down to St. Simmons island. It was the first time I ever tried marijuana. We went off on the island and smoked it and got high. We ended up getting caught, but I got out of a school suspension. Sooner or later, my mother said, we will just take you out of school and you can get your GED. I went for a little while but she didn't push me to go.

So, I got a job and started to make money and buy drugs. I was hanging around the wrong crowd, meeting friends at their houses and getting high after work. But I noticed this one family that moved next to us. They went to a small United Pentecostal Church.

They looked so different: they had a glow about them. They

became my friends. Bobby and I used to play backyard football. Eventually, I went to a religious revival. Brother Stern preached, and God spoke through him to me. I was convinced but went home and kept on partying. I remember drinking a whole bottle of vodka I found under Mom's sink. I replaced it with water. I remember at my workplace I bought a little bag of acid. I took it and was up for three days straight. And then I smoked a joint.

The next thing I knew I was overdosing. I fell on the ground and told God, I will serve you. Forgive me, I said as I crawled on the grass outside. Then I was in the hospital where they checked me and did what they needed to do to make sure I was okay.

That Wednesday night, I brought all my bad music CDs and my marijuana t-shirt to the United Pentecostal Church. I was there thirty minutes early sitting on the steps before it started. I said to the

Pastor, Brother Camlic, "You can burn these. I'm ready to get baptized." He baptized me in the name of Jesus. God filled me with the Holy Ghost and I spoke in tongues.

That week I brought my mom to church along with my brother. Eventually they both got baptized and God filled both of them with the Holy Ghost. At the time, my mother was dating her boyfriend, Chuck. I remember the night he called me and said he wasn't feeling good, so I left to see him.

I immediately went to where he was and I laid my hands on him while praying. God instantly healed him. I baptized him in God's name, and God filled him with the Holy Ghost.

I started to become addicted to Soulwinning. All of Hell was attacking me spiritually, but I wasn't going allow the demons to stop me. People in the church were teaching me Bible studies, and I was growing in God. So I went back to work. All my friends saw a change in me. I was walking around with my Bible, witnessing to everyone I could.

My brother caught the fire and went to a soulwinners bootcamp down in St. Petersburg, Florida. I wanted to go so bad, but my mother couldn't afford to send me. Someone in the church blessed my brother. I did whatever I could to go the following year. I ended up

going to eight of them altogether.
This is where the story begins.

# Chapter 2:
# It Starts with
# Intimacy

It all starts in this chapter. If you want to be led by the spirit to win souls, you've got to be connected to the source. You can have so much passion to win souls like I have. But at times in my life, I let my passion outweigh my intimacy with the Lord.

I personally won over 75 people to Jesus Christ. To God be the glory for every last soul. The word "intimacy" means close familiarity or friendship—closeness. An intimate relationship is an interpersonal relationship that involves physical or emotional intimacy.

Daniel 11:32 (KJVS) says, "And such as do wickedly against the covenant shall he corrupt by flatteries: but the people that do know their God shall be strong, and do exploits." The word for "know in Hebrew is ‫לְהַכִּיר‬.

It means to recognize, know, find out, make out, ascertain, understand. Does God recognize you? Has he seen your face?

When was the last time we sought him for him and not just when we needed something? When he recognizes you, the Bible says you will be strong and do exploits. It's time to slow down and stop praying for souls all the time and get to know Jesus.

Once you are intimate with him, you become pregnant when the word gets in you. When you are pregnant, there are spiritual babies in the womb, and souls will be born through intimacy. It's like false insemination if you try to go out and just win souls without the intimacy.

Matthew 7:21-22 (KJVS) says, "Not everyone that saith unto me, Lord, Lord, shall enter into the kingdom of heaven; but he that doeth the will of my Father which is in heaven. Many will say to me in that day, Lord, Lord, have we not prophesied in thy name? and in thy name have cast out devils? and in thy name done many wonderful works?"

Jesus is talking about the people of the name here. Is it possible these people in Matthew 7 were so busy with ministry that Jesus didn't recognize them.

I was so busy trying to win every last soul on fire coming back from that first bootcamp. I didn't know how to rest at all. I was on the go until I burned out. I let my passion outweigh the intimacy.

God would have made you an angel if he didn't want you to rest. The reason most of us don't know how to rest is because we don't know how to come out of the warfare. The warfare will wear you out. No one can stay in the warfare 24/7. Even Jesus pulled away for solitude and prayer. This is what most of us have missed.

The warfare is empowered by the love affair. The Bible says to resist the devil and he will flee now. That's warfare. To resist, I need strength. Where do I get that strength from? The joy of the Lord is my strength. I get the strength from the joy. Where do I get the joy from? In his presence is the fullness. I have the joy that gives me the strength to resist the devil from the presence.

The reason why soulwinning isn't working for some people is given in the Bible. Luke 5:5 says, "And Simon answering, said unto him, Master, we have toiled all the night, and have taken nothing: nevertheless at thy word I will let down the net."

You cannot win souls without Jesus. The reason Jesus isn't allowing your soulwinning adventures to work is because you're convinced you know the correct way to do things. Imagine if a husband and a wife just wanted to have kids without a relationship of intimacy. So why are you wanting to win souls without intimacy?

Are you afraid like I was? If I don't win souls, then I will go to hell. That was my thinking. I would walk around seeing all these church people who weren't winning souls. I thought they are all going to go to hell. I was wrong. I'll explain more in the next chapter.

# Chapter 3:
# Be Apostolic

When you hear the word "apostolic," what goes through your head? They only way to get the depth of this word is to look into the story of what the apostles did. Now, don't say that their work was only for them. It's for you as well.

Acts 2:46-47 (KJVS) says, "And they, continuing daily with one accord in the temple, and breaking bread from house to house, did eat their meat with gladness and singleness of heart, praising God, and having favor with all the people. And the Lord added to the church daily such as should be saved."

So, you are telling me the Apostles went to church and got fed, and then they left their service and went house to house. That's how the church should be, and the Bible says the Lord added to the church daily as such should be saved.

If you are not doing what the Apostles did, how can you even be apostolic? Jesus ate with sinners. I am truly convinced that we should hear cursing and smell like smoke and alcohol. When is the last time you took a sinncr out for dinner and listened to him?

I don't know about you, but I'm sick and tired of the Professional

Pentecostal church. I have been to eight soulwinners bootcamps, came home, and went back to a normal service. I've been there, through the motions. We need to be the most aggressive church in town.

If you don't have visitors In your church, I believe it's the will of God to shut your service down so you get into the streets and take this gospel house to house. I'm tired of preaching to you. Get me some sinners I can love.

We have the best singers in the world and the best preachers in the world, but the hidden talent is inside the church that needs to get into the city. People will knock the doors down if they felt what we felt. But the question is, are we too stingy to tell anyone about it?

I am truly convinced that if you hold a license to preach or evangelize, you must attend a Soulwinners Bootcamp with Brother Maddix. How can I have a church if I can't even fill it up? Billy

Cole said, you are a soulwinner before you are a preacher.

Soulwinning isn't a ministry in the church: it is the Ministry of Jesus Christ. Everyone who has the Holy Ghost needs to be intimate with Jesus and he will use you to win souls. Everyone isn't going to get on board, but the ones truly following Jesus will back you up. Jesus said, "My sheep shall hear my voice." Jesus started with 4,000 and ended up with 12. They left because they rejected Jesus.

There is no Joy in your city if the Apostolic Church remains isolated. There were two churches in the book of Acts. We always talk about the church that had revival and hit the streets. But if you look at Acts 8, the church that stayed isolated went to prison. It's time to be the most aggressive church in town. How big is your city? Think about this:

1.68 people die per second

101 people die per minute

6048 people die per hour

145 thousand people die per day

53 million people die per year

Here we go, Generation Z. I want you to be a giant killer after you grasp this and read this book. This is for you. Let's stop letting the world entertain us. It's time to live.

In Matthew 3:11 (KJVS), John the Baptist says to his followers, "I baptize you with water unto repentance: but he that cometh after me is mightier than I, whose shoes I am not worthy to bear. He shall baptize you with the Holy Ghost, and with fire.

Generation Z, that fire will keep you intoxicated with Jesus. I have to have Jesus when I wake up. I've got to have His Word. I've got to witness to someone. God will lead you. When I go to school, I'm going to start a Bible study group. Stop inviting people to church. Take church to them, go house to house and they will follow you as you follow Jesus.

Come on! I'm getting fired up as grasp this truth. I know you can't wait to put this book down and get you some sinners to hang out with. When I first was in church, I went to this skatepark and started to hang out with some people.

I was moved with compassion because I knew some of the kids were hungry. I went and picked up a pizza and blessed them. I told them where I attend church. This kid came and checked it out because I showed interest in him. Be apostolic.

Another time, we were having a revival and I felt the burden to get some people there. I remember going to Office Depot where I made 50 flyers. I then went door to door and from that effort, one guy came, and he is still serving God today. In your face, Devil!

There is the story of John "Red" Fuller. He was burglarizing a home. The owner came home unexpectedly. John Fuller was spooked and turned around with the gun he was holding. He shot her and killed her. He was the baddest man in prison. He ordered the execution of other prisoners. Everyone was terrified of John Fuller.

He was red-headed so they called him "Red." He also had shed a lot of blood. John "Red" Fuller was one of the strongest men in the nation. He had the flu and could bench press 425 pounds and was apologizing, "I'm so sorry that I couldn't do more."

He was a fierce individual. No one wanted to do anything with him. But there was an old blind preacher who would go preach at Brushy Mountain Prison, and he would routinely ask where John Fuller was. He would say, "Lead me to John Fuller." Thank God for blind preachers who don't see what everyone else sees. He refused to consider what everyone else focused on. People like the blind preacher refuse to be intimidated at what everyone else is intimidated by. And this old blind preacher who walked into Brushy Mountain Prison would routinely ask, "Would someone lead me to John Red Fuller?" So, they would take him to his cell and John Red Fuller didn't want anything to do with the old blind preacher.

And the blind preacher would say the same thing every time, "God is gonna fill you, John Red Fuller, with the Holy Ghost." Fuller would curse the preacher and tell him to get lost. "I don't want to see you anymore! Get out of here!" The next week the old blind preacher came back. He said, "God is gonna fill you with the gift of the Holy Ghost."

The preacher was operating with the gift of prophecy. John Fuller was told by a lot of people that he was a killer and murderer. People told him he was no good. There was nothing God could do for him and no one loved him. His mom didn't love him. His dad didn't love him.

God didn't love him. That's what others told him.

This preacher was telling him, "God is gonna fill you with the Holy Ghost." That prophecy was warring against false prophecy; week after week it was the same routine. "God is gonna fill you with the Holy Ghost." But Fuller always responded the same, "Get lost preacher!" Eventually one day, that prophecy got ahold of John Red Fuller and started dealing with his heart. He came to hear preaching at a meeting one night.

His heart wasn't right, but something got ahold of him. You know what I'm talking about. Anyone who has been there before knows when there is no hope. But somebody keeps telling you that Jesus saves. Sure enough, God did fill him with the Holy Ghost and he was baptized in the name of Jesus Christ.

An old blind preacher had a package for him. He said, "I been waiting to give this to you." In the package was a Bible that said, "Reverend John Red Fuller." John Red Fuller was licensed to preach the gospel in prison by the United Pentecostal Church. It was a profound life change and the prison paroled him. He came out of prison and preached the gospel of Jesus Christ all over the nation. As this chapter closes, please don't go back and be a Professional Pentecostal. Instead be a Apostolic world changer!

# Chapter 4:
# My Darkest Night

I'm going get real in this chapter.
It's time to jump into my shoes and
feel all the disappointment I have
had and all the heartache I have
endured. You will see what I am
now and what I been through. I am
happily married with two children.
I am the only one who works. My

profession is a truck driver. I'm home once through the week and on weekends.

I have had the Holy Ghost for nineteen years and through all of these years, I have had my disappointments and heartaches. At times I have held onto a thread of faith. It feels like I have been through the ringer. I have been all across the states. I stopped to write this book because I want to impact someone's life, just as God has impacted mine.

It was at the beginning of 2019 when a spiritual hurricane hit me like a freight train. I remember as if it just happened yesterday. I was driving through Texas, near Odessa, when the spirit of fear hit me hard. It was so hard that I literally pulled my truck over at a rest area. I had anxiety and fear all over me.

I got out of my truck and started to pray. I didn't know what to do but call on the name of Jesus. I worshiped God but I still felt it. I remember the story of Job. The devil had to get permission to touch Job. I'm truly convinced that the devil got permission to touch me.

I got into my truck and drove my way to Phoenix, Arizona. I made it to Demning, New Mexico. I got out of my truck and went inside a restaurant for a salad. I thought I was having a stroke. fear was all over me. I called my family and told them to pray as I called for an ambulance. I got checked out and all my vital signs were good on the EKGs.

Some policemen took me back to my truck. I carried on the next day as if the spirit of fear still tormented me. The next day I took a vacation in Phoenix and went to watch LSU play in the Fiesta Bowl. I had first row tickets. I sat there and watched the game. After halftime, the spirit hit me so hard.

I literally went to the middle of the arena and got help. I was having a panic attack. My mouth was going dry as I was calling on Jesus. It seemed to take forever to get help. I literally thought Jesus was about to take me. I went downstairs to a special room set up for players.

I got checked again before an ambulance came and got me. I went to the hospital and got dye shot through my veins to see if I had any blockages. Everything checked out. I ubered back to my truck. I eventually made it home a few days later. I made it to church still fighting this spirit that had attacked me. At times my face would tingle with my leg while I was being affected by the spirit pf fear. I tried to worship God. I eventually came off the road and worked locally. I remember that months went by as I dealt with this spirit.

One night at work it got so bad that I was about to go home. I remember telling God, please I can't handle this anymore. Get rid of it. Immediately, I felt the peace of God sweep over me as the spirit left. I was worshipping God and thanking him.

I don't know why I had to endure my darkest night. The closer you get to Jesus the more suffering you will endure. Through my darkest hour, I had grown closer to Jesus. Get as close as you can to Jesus so he can do something for you. The closer you get, the more clearly you can hear him.

# Chapter 5: Pioneers of the Faith Quotes

Here are some Heroes of the Faith Quotes that have deeply influenced my life:

*Save them all and let God sort them out.* --Wayne Huntley.

*The greatest church in your city is a church that serves your city.* --Matt Maddix.

*Preaching doesn't build great churches, but great soulwinners do.* --Marrell Cornwell

*If you don't use the Holy Ghost, give it back cause it cost too much.* --Vesta Mangun.

*If you reach for the people nobody wants, God will send you the people everybody wants.* --Matt Maddix.

*God can only do what you got faith for.* --David Smith.

*We make Heroes out of our Soulwinners cause there very few.* --Wayne Huntley

*My Destiny is greater than my disaster.* -- Jeff Arnold.

*The treasure is in the field and the coin is in the fish's mouth.* --Matt Maddix.

*Catch on fire and others will love to come watch you burn.* --John Wesley

*Give me 100 preachers who fear nothing but sin and desire nothing but God; such alone will shake the gates of hell.* --John Wesley

*The chief danger of the 20th century will be religion without the Holy Spirit, Christianity without Christ, forgiveness without repentance, salvation without regeneration, politics without God, and heaven without hell.* --William Booth

*Most Christians would like to send their recruits to Bible college for five years. I would like to send them to hell for five minutes. That would do more*

than anything else to prepare them for a lifetime of compassionate ministry. -- William Booth

*In your face, Devil.* --Matt Maddix

*Some men's passion is for gold. Some men's passion is for art. Some men's passion is for fame. My passion is for souls.* --William Booth

*Everyone needs a Judas in their life to crucify them.* --Wayne Huntley

*You don't get good to get God; you get God and then get Good.* --Matt Maddix.

# Chapter 6:
# The Outreach That Will
# Win the Whole City

I am fired up just thinking about reaching the lost. I'm ready for you to tell me what works. Okay, hang on a moment. Prayer works. Intimacy with Christ works. Here it goes! Now, are you ready?

Have a blessing the community service. Faith is spelled like this: W-O-R-K. It will cost you to reach the lost. Go out and buy iPads and bikes, and give away food. Hand out vouchers for electricity, Walmart gift cards, money, etc. Buy thousands of bright yellow door hangers. Put Invitation on them with blessing the the community service this Sunday on them. If you need a sample email me at erwin7022@gmail.com

Use black bold letters and a picture of the prizes on them along with the address. Where we mess up is putting religious stuff on the door hanger. The day before, go out and hang them on doors around the city. It's up to you if the bus is running.

Now don't be surprised if 100 or 300 people show up. Have someone up front registering people as they walk in. No, the church members don't register. Have a service. Pray and seek God as to how he wants the service to go. Spirit led soulwinning is the key.

At the end, have an altar call and make everyone come up to the front. How do you do that? What works? Okay. Ask how many of y'all want to go to heaven: raise your hands? Hands go up. How many want to go to hell? Raise your hands. No hands besides the crazy ones, maybe.

How many of y'all have been baptized? You remember, this is when the preacher says, "Now I baptize you in the name of the father, the son and the Holy Ghost." Raise your hands if you've been baptized. Hands go up everywhere because that's how the church world baptizes.

You say, that's awesome. I got good news and bad news. The bad news is that no one in the entire Bible was ever baptized while the preacher repeated "the Father, the Son, and the Holy Ghost." But I got some good news for you. Everyone in the Bible was baptized in the name of Jesus. The Bible says, do every word or deed in the name of Jesus. Baptism is an action. It's a deed. Raise your hands if you want to be baptized in Jesus' name. Have your church people raise their hands. Shout and worship.

I have never ever seen this not work. I been all across the world with soulwinners, at bootcamps, and hanging around Tim Downs. The fastest growing city should have the fastest growing churches.

Please don't sit there and say God is gonna send me 200 people. I'm just gonna sit here and wait on God because he said in the Bible to wait on the Lord. That word "wait" means to serve the Lord.

We had a service like this at the church I attend in Dalton. We had 70 new visitors and baptized 17 people from that revival during that month. Yes, I had to work hard. No, you are not gonna keep everyone, but some will stay.

# Chapter 7:
# Beware
# Fire Extinguishers

Have you ever seen a dog bark at a parked car? Have you ever heard the phrase, the pigeons are looking for statues? What I'm trying to say is, beware of the people who try to put your fire out.

You can probably think of people right now who are negative or maybe they don't join you in your soulwinning adventure. You are not alone. Jesus called Peter a devil for trying to stop him from taking the cross to the world.

Religious people crucified Jesus. These religious people didn't believe Jesus. When fisherman aren't fishing, they are fussing and fighting, trying to find fault with one another across the church aisles.

Stop pointing your fingers and follow Jesus. Build a church around the fire extinguishers. Turn your new converts into soulwinning machines. Don't get distracted. Our churches should be the most aggressive in town.

Our carpets should have stains on them and pews should be dirty. We should have dirty altars. It's time for standing room only in church.

You are trying to get everyone on board for outreach. Until people catch the vision, you want everyone.

Set a fire and some will join while the other ones observe. Don't get distracted by ministries. You are not in competition with them.

I have carried a large load where I felt all alone before. Yes, it discourages you. You will never go any higher than your leadership is willing to go.

Don't give up. That's where prayer comes in. Start worshiping God as the leadership reaches higher. Stay committed. I have never seen a dead soulwinning church. You've got to protect the new converts. It's time to surround them with love.

It is what it is. I left my church a few times cause my leadership wasn't going any higher. I felt stuck. As I and a few others were the only ones carrying the burden to get everyone on board, it was a difficult time. Yes, this is the raw, uncut version of me being me.

I served in Atlanta with Brother Downs, one of the most powerful Soulwinner's ever. I went on this mission in Detroit with the Giunta's to one of the worst city's in America.

To learn how to have a successful outreach, I will go deeper in the next chapter. I slept in the pastor's basement while my family was back home. I went and got a job and my own place as my family joined me. I have been mentored by Lee Fowler. I could go to any city in America and find a church. I say that in fear of the Almighty God.

What are your secrets? I will unleash this fire too. Are you ready?

I remember going to Ashland, Kentucky, to a bootcamp and sleeping in my car. I just got there and experienced another bootcamp. I drove wherever I could for the mission. I mastered the Heaven or Hell method from Brother Downs.

I moved back to Dalton with my family. I learned the ministry mindset in the worst cities in America. I went out and bought a Bluebird bus. I filled it with all kinds of sinners. The Bible says, unless the Lord builds the house, we labor in vain.

I had it in my mind to beware of the fire extinguishers. Why had I come back to Dalton? Thoughts were running through my mind: the sweet people here, the great pastor I had here. I didn't have everyone on board when it came to outreach. I believe in every church in America. The Pastor should lead right next to the outreach director.

Pass the addiction down of soulwinning to the ministry. Get

ahold of it, Pastor! Come on, Sunday school teachers! Catch the fire saint. It's your time. It's time to get addicted now.

# Chapter 8:
# Spirit Led Soulwinning

The apostle Paul says in Romans 8:14 (KJVS), "For as many as are led by the Spirit of God, they are the sons of God." How do I know when it's time to win someone? Where do I start? Have you ever thought these thoughts? I have often asked myself, where do I start in my city?

I lived in a big apartment complex. I had this burning desire. It was like a urgency. The thought of going to bless people in my apartment complex wouldn't go away. I saw myself doing it before I actually did it.

I'd get in my vehicle and head to the foodbank to load my vehicle down. I knocked on every door and started to bless people. I came to this one door and knocked. I introduced myself and asked if they needed any food.

I asked them if they had ever been baptized in Jesus' name. The lady's eyes got big and she said, "You baptize in Jesus' name." I said, "Yes ma'am, we do." She replied, "I have been looking for a church that baptizes in Jesus' name." She eventually came and we baptized her as her whole family watched.

Don't ignore the voice of God when it comes time to be led by the

Spirit. Another time, I was at work being a light to people. I come to find out that the second shift boss has a tumor in his throat from vaping.

I was so full of fire and the Holy Ghost. The Lord spoke to me and said, "Son, he is about to get a miracle." Then I asked the man if it was okay to pray. He said, "Yes, it wouldn't hurt." I replied, "Jesus, I bind this tumor and lose this miracle in Jesus' name."

As weeks and months go by, and I see the man had returned to work. I asked him what the doctor said. The tumor had shrunk and eventually it went away completely. We must be led by the spirit to do things for God.

I was traveling in my vehicle around Knoxville, Tennessee. I stopped in Maryville to go to church. I got out of my vehicle outside the grocery store. I saw these two elderly ladies. I started to feel the burden to talk to them.

I asked them if they had ever received the Holy Ghost, and they said, yes. Then I said, "That's awesome! What was your experience like?" They said that they both accepted the Lord as their personal savior. I said, "That's awesome!"

I told them my experience of receiving the Holy Ghost. I spoke in tongues. I asked if God wanted to fill you all with the Holy Ghost today, would you want it? They said yes, and so we started to ask Jesus to forgive us of our sins.

I said to them, "As soon as I lay my hands on your heads, you will speak in tongues. By the authority of the word of God and by the power of the name of Jesus, receive the Holy Ghost." In the next five minutes, they started to speak in tongues. I called the pastor in that town.

He came over to the parking lot and introduced himself to them. After the service, he took me in his office and said, "You answered my prayer today. I was just talking to the General Superintendent, Brother Bernard, about how he would like some elderly people to get the Holy Ghost." If you are led by the spirit, you will win souls.

Another time I was working a job and I started to witness to a guy. I told him my testimony. We started talking about baptism. He knew what the Bible said about baptism, but he didn't really understand it in detail.

He thought that we must repeat Mathew 28:19 when getting baptized. His friend was about to baptize him that way, but he hesitated. I showed him Acts 2:38. So he said, I'm gonna pray and ask God to confirm it.

A few weeks passed and he called me up and said, "When I drove into my trailer with my forklift, I looked on the wall and it said Acts 2:38." He said, "Will you baptize me?" I said, "Yes, I will!" I met him at the church and baptized him in the name of Jesus, and God filled him with the Holy Ghost. This is spirit led soulwinning.

# Chapter 9:
# Don't Be Condemned
# If You Are Not
# Winning Souls

The Bible says that we are measured by our worship, not by how many souls we win to Christ.

Genesis 15:1 (KJVS) says, "After these things, the word of the Lord came unto Abram in a vision, saying, 'Fear not, Abram. I am thy shield, and thy exceeding great reward.'"

Who is your great reward, Abraham? The Lord said "I am." Isn't the Lord greater than the soul? John 3:17 (KJVS) says, "For God sent not his Son into the world to condemn the world; but that the world through him might be saved."

Jesus didn't come to condemn you. He came to build you up. He believes in you. Stop condemning yourself. When you are in a love affair with Christ, souls will be born. I use to walk around condemning myself if I wasn't winning souls.

Then I looked at other saints and started to condemn them. We are measured by our worship, not by how many souls we won. You must be spirit led to win souls, and you must not have a mind of confusion.

There is a story of this man of God who was in his car at a stop sign. He said, "I'm going to go to the hospital, God." And God told him to go to the park. "I'm gonna go to the hospital, God." The Lord said, "You go to the hospital but I will be at the park." The moral of the story is that you've got to be where God is already working in your city.

First of all, you have to believe in yourself. Speak faith to see the power of God activated in your life. I will get this raise. I am gonna be successful at this diet. I am blessed and highly favored. Now, you feel good about yourself. No negative figure of speech is to come from your mouth. Watch what you speak to yourself and others.

Now you feel good about yourself. At this point you understand condemnation. You understand intimacy. That word "know" sticks to you now. Have I been up in the Lord's bedroom today before I even tried to condemn myself?

As hard as I try to condemn myself, it doesn't work because I am full of the Holy Ghost. Look at this passage of scripture in John 10:27 (KJVS): "My sheep hear my voice, and I know them, and they follow me." Wow, now you can clearly hear his voice which makes this chapter even better.

I am on top of the world now. Jesus and I are one; we are working together. I feel like Peter with the keys to the kingdom. Let's go, Jesus. Let's tell everyone about you. Jesus pulls you by the collar and says, "Sit here and spend time with me." The word says to preach the Gospel to every creature where you go in the streets.

Well, that's where I have been for a while. We win more souls to Jesus when we are connected and don't feel condemned.

www.ingramcontent.com/pod-product-compliance
Lightning Source LLC
Chambersburg PA
CBHW070636120726

47909CB00004B/1465